A chart setting forth the first voyage of Christopher Columbus.

Route of voyage.

The Canary
Who Sailed
With Columbus

By Susan Wiggs

Illustrated by
Sharon Loy Anderson

PANDA BOOKS ★ Austin, Texas

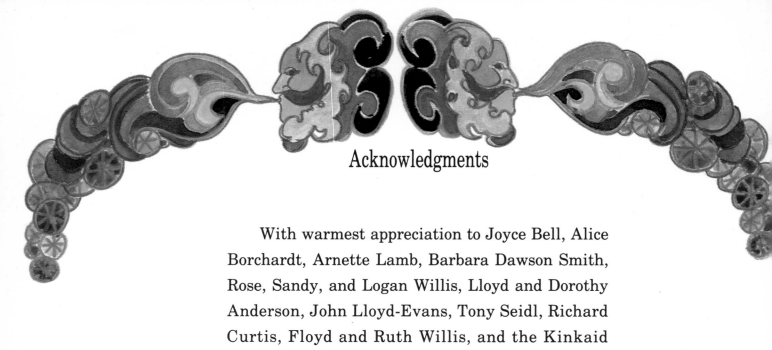

Acknowledgments

With warmest appreciation to Joyce Bell, Alice Borchardt, Arnette Lamb, Barbara Dawson Smith, Rose, Sandy, and Logan Willis, Lloyd and Dorothy Anderson, John Lloyd-Evans, Tony Seidl, Richard Curtis, Floyd and Ruth Willis, and the Kinkaid School for their help and encouragement.

Library of Congress Cataloging-in-Publication Data

Wiggs, Susan.
   The canary who sailed with Columbus / by Susan Wiggs : illustrated by Sharon Loy Anderson.
     p.   cm.
   Summary: Carlos the canary accompanies Columbus on his voyage to the new world.
   ISBN 0-89015-719-7 : $12.95
   [1. Canaries — Fiction. 2. Birds — Fiction. 3. Columbus, Christopher — Fiction. 4. America — Discovery and exploration — Spanish — Fiction.]
   I. Anderson, Sharon Loy, ill. II. Title.
PZ7.W6388Can   1989
[E]--dc20   89-8821
                                           CIP
                                           AC

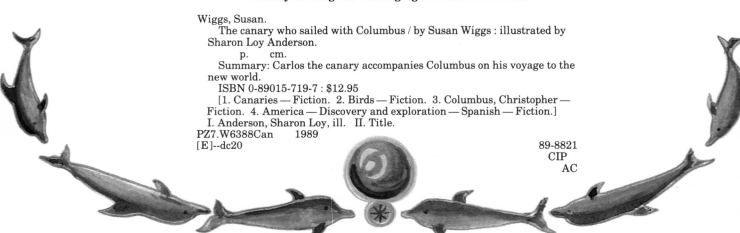

FIRST EDITION

Published in the United States of America
By Panda Books
An Imprint of Eakin Publications, Inc.
P.O. Drawer 90159   ★   Austin, TX 78709-0159

ISBN 0-89015-719-7

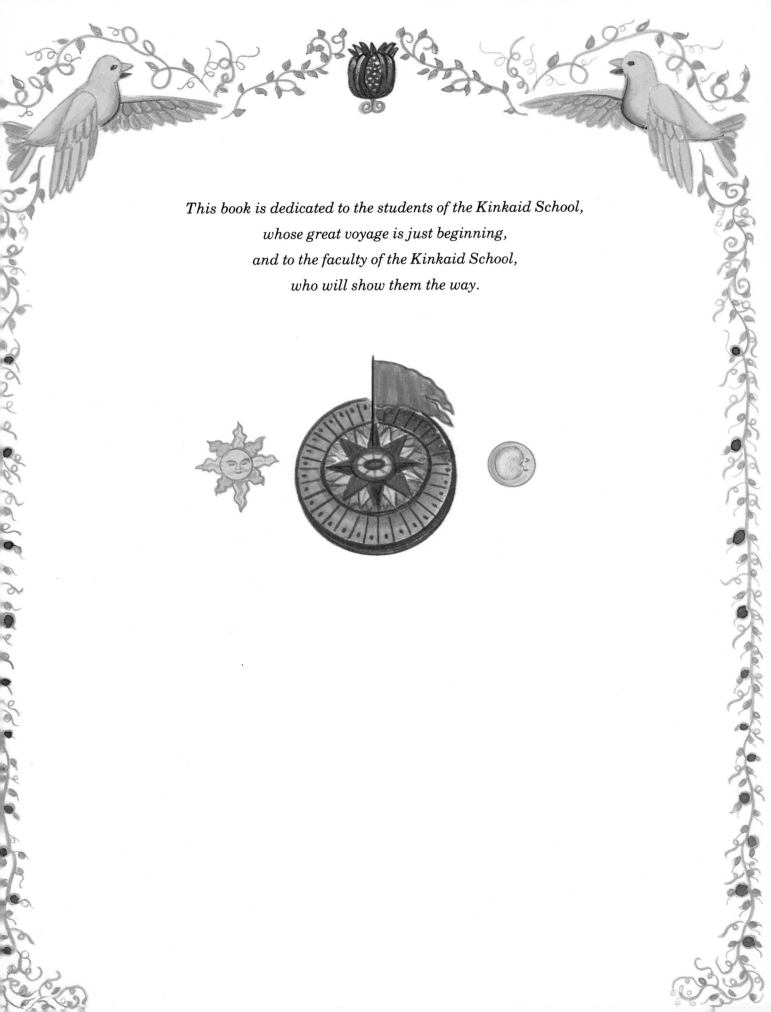

This book is dedicated to the students of the Kinkaid School,
whose great voyage is just beginning,
and to the faculty of the Kinkaid School,
who will show them the way.

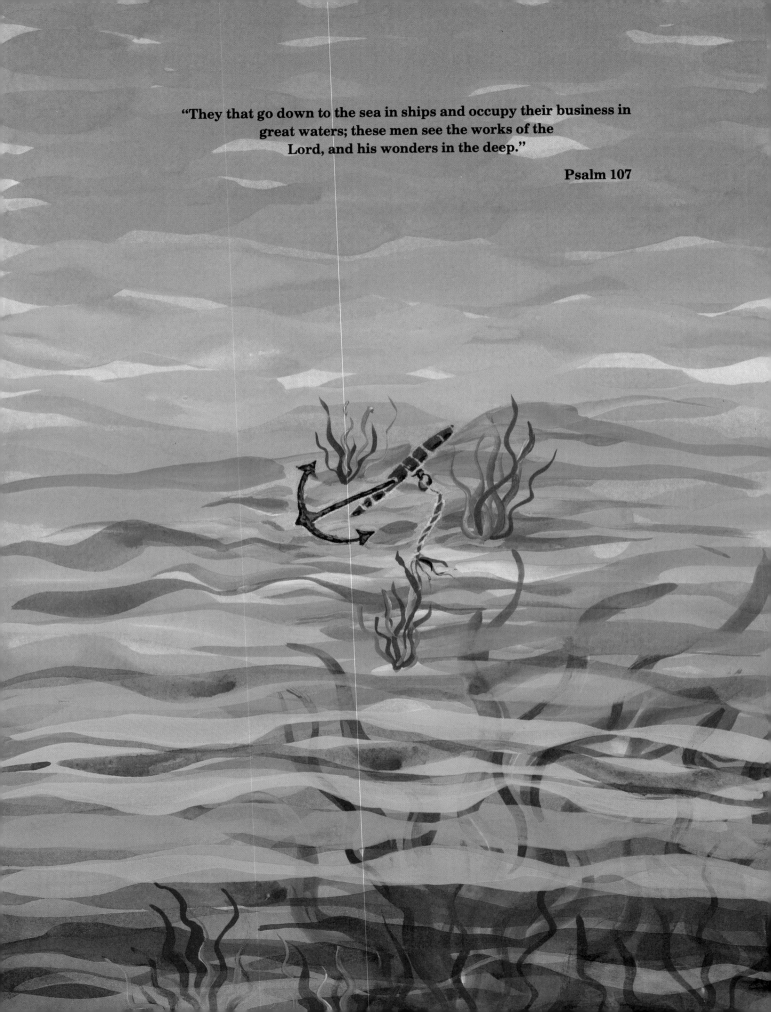

"They that go down to the sea in ships and occupy their business in great waters; these men see the works of the Lord, and his wonders in the deep."

Psalm 107

Gabrielo was a cobbler, old and poor, who lived in the port city of Palos in Spain. Carlos was his canary, yellow and bright, who kept him company day after day.

Each morning when the sun rose, Carlos lifted his voice in bright, liquid song and trilled the hours away. From his perch by the window he could watch the fishing boats, *caravelas,* and *latinas* at the wharf. Gabrielo sat at his workbench, his hammer tapping as he mended shoes.

But as time passed, old Gabrielo's eyes grew weak, and the work began to tire him. The bell over the doorway hung silent, for customers took their shoes elsewhere. Some nights Gabrielo and Carlos went to bed with empty bellies.

On the second day of August in the Year of Our Lord 1492, the bell over the doorway jingled. The dusty white light of a Spanish summer streamed into the shop. Carlos flitted to Gabrielo's shoulder and watched expectantly.

In walked a tall, silver-haired man with eyes as blue as the ocean and a voice that rang with hearty humor.

"I am Christopher Columbus," he said. "Admiral of the Ocean Sea. Will you mend my boot?"

Carlos flapped his butter-yellow wings and flew across the shop, the better to see this great man, whose arrival in Palos had caused such a stir among the sailors and fishermen.

"Of course I'll mend your boot," said Gabrielo.

While the cobbler plied his hammer, Columbus spun a tale. "Queen Isabella has granted me three worthy ships and ninety stout-hearted men. Tomorrow we set sail to find a westward route to the Indies."

Gabrielo chuckled and Carlos chirped. "A westward route?" the old cobbler asked. "But the Indies lie far to the east."

Columbus's laughter boomed like summer thunder. He took a pumice stone from the workbench and tossed it in his big, strong hand. "The world is oval, like this stone. By San Fernando! A man needs only the courage and heart to sail west with the wind, and he will reach Cipango, Cathay, the Orient."

Gabrielo cut a piece of leather for the sole of the boot. "It sounds like a long and dangerous adventure. Why do you undertake it?"

"For glory!" Columbus shouted, and his eyes shone like two stars in the night sky. "Glory and gold!"

Carlos hopped excitedly from table to perch. "Glory and gold," he chirped. "Glory and gold!"

Columbus laughed. "Aye, my golden lad, and to see new lands, new peoples, new wonders. To dine on rare fruits with sultans, to see ladies draped in brocade, to smell the spices of Malabar on the wind."

He put out a finger and Carlos alighted on it, his heart tripping.

"What a fine fellow you are," said Columbus, setting Carlos on his shoulder. "Your song is like sunshine. What say you, little friend? Would you like to come with me on my great voyage of discovery?"

Carlos stopped his flapping and chirping. Gabrielo stopped his tapping and clipping. Looking hale and handsome as a man of great destiny, Columbus planted his hands on his hips.

"You offer a fine opportunity," said Gabrielo. "I am growing old, and can no longer support my little canary. Perhaps it would be good for him to sail west with the wind."

Columbus nodded. "I would like to bring this happy little fellow along as my mascot. I shall give you a hundred *maravedis* for him."

Carlos blinked. A hundred *maravedis*! Old Gabrielo could live like King Ferdinand on a hundred *maravedis*! He hopped up and down on the great broad shoulder of Christopher Columbus and chirped, "West with the wind! Glory and gold!"

"Very well," said Gabrielo. "You may take my little bird. But watch over him carefully. Let no harm befall him. God speed you on your voyage."

Carlos fluttered with excitement, although he saw sadness in Gabrielo's eyes. The cobbler would be lonely with no little canary-bird to sing to him. But at least Gabrielo would no longer go hungry.

At dawn the next day, people lined the docks of the seaport. Women threw flowers into the water, men cheered, and robed friars chanted prayers for the voyagers. The flagship *Santa Maria* slipped down the Rio Tinto and out into the vast blue waters of the sea. Carlos felt proud and brave to be joining the Admiral on his great voyage of discovery.

The one thing he didn't like was Don Gato, the ship's cat. Black as midnight and sneaky as morning fog, Don Gato prowled the decks and waited to swipe those long, sharp claws at Carlos. "The Indies," hissed Don Gato. "I don't think we'll find the Indies. I think we'll sail off the edge of the world."

"You are foolish to believe those old superstitions," scolded Carlos.

Like a streak of black lightning, the cat's forepaw slashed out. A wicked claw stabbed into one of Carlos's tailfeathers. Chirping frantically, he flew away. But a sharp pain told him he'd left that feather behind. His heart beating fast, he perched on a yardarm that Don Gato was too lazy to climb.

Warm trade winds carried the *Santa Maria* and her sister ships, *Nina* and *Pinta*, over rolling green and blue swells, onward, westward. By day, Carlos soared up into the full sails, through the rigging, and flew with the boatswain-birds and chirping kestrels. At night, with Don Gato locked safely outside, he ate seeds from the Admiral's hand and slept on a perch in the cabin.

One balmy day Columbus called to Carlos. "We've reached the Canary Islands," he said with a jolly laugh. "I think your grandsires must have come from here many years ago."

"Just what we need," snarled Don Gato, who lay in the shade of a ship's boat. "More canaries."

Carlos ignored the cat. He hopped up and down with joy when he saw the lofty green islands, crowned by stone castles and creased by deep ravines. From across the water, he heard the songs of his kin.

But the Canary Islands were not the destination for the Admiral of the
Ocean Sea, and he stayed only long enough to mend the rudder of the *Pinta*
and to change the rigging of the *Nina*.

"Weigh anchor!" shouted Columbus. "Hoist the main course! Onward! Sing farewell to your kin, Carlos, for we sail west with the wind!"

Weeks passed, and Carlos grew accustomed to life under sail. He saw the vast, thick sargasso weeds which choked the sea and frightened the sailors. He smelled the cool fragrance of dew drying from the sails when the sun came up. He heard the regular call of the sandglass boy, turning his *ampolleta* and singing out the hour:

> *One glass is gone*
> *and now the second floweth;*
> *more shall run down*
> *if my God willeth.*

Columbus knew the way of a ship in the midst of the sea. He navigated by "dead reckoning," keeping account of direction, wind speed, time, and distance.

"The men do not know how far we have come," said the Admiral to Carlos one night. His brow creased with worry, Columbus wrote in his log. "We're running out of food and water. Carlos, they might turn against me if we don't sight land soon."

"Columbus is just trying to make himself a great lord," grumbled Don Gato. He gnawed a fishbone with his sharp teeth. "If the crew rebels, I'll have you for dessert, bird."

Carlos gave a fearful chirp.

"Perhaps I was wrong," said Columbus. "Perhaps I should have left you home, safe in the cobbler's shop."

"We'll starve," snarled Don Gato, "and all because of the mad fantasy of this Genoese man."

While singing a soothing song for the Admiral, Carlos wondered what old Gabrielo was doing. Did he miss his little canary? Was he lonely in his dusty, silent shop?

But just as his heart began to ache, Carlos saw, with his sharp little bird's eyes, a distant glimmer of light outside the portal. He cocked his head.

Columbus asked, "What do you see?"

Carlos chirped wildly and flew out to the deck. "By San Fernando," said the Admiral, "it looks like a little candle rising and falling. Go and see what it is, Carlos."

"And don't come back" sneered Don Gato.

Carlos took wing, flying west with the wind to see if the white glimmer could really be land. The big, dark shadow of a herring gull swept over him, but Carlos flew bravely onward, westward.

At dawn on October 12, 1492, the light became a hazy bump, piled like a cloud on the horizon. The hazy bump became a sand-baked island, sitting like an emerald in calm waters.

Carlos swooped down and plucked a twig from the top of a tree.

Beating his wings fast, he returned to the *Santa Maria*. He flew joyfully around the Admiral, who laughed at his antics.

"What is it, little Carlos? Why do you fly around me so?"
Carlos dropped the twig into the Admiral's hand. "Land!" sang Carlos.
"Land! Land!"

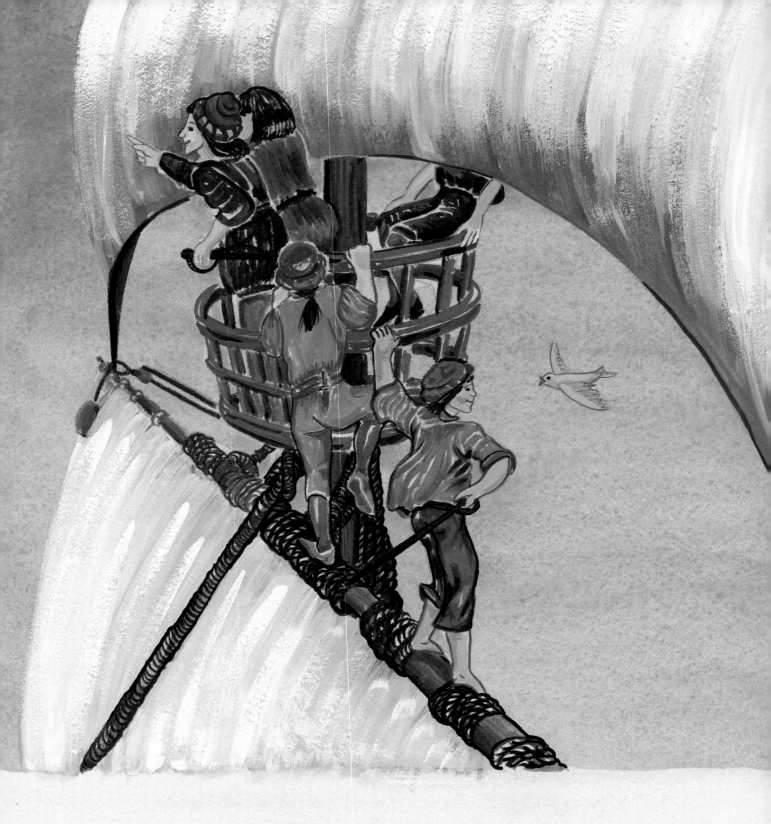

Men scrambled up the rigging and shaded their eyes. A sailor on the *Pinta* cried, *"Tierra!"* A seaman fired a lombard.

Columbus went to the rail and squinted at the horizon. "Thanks be to God! We have reached the other side of the Ocean Sea!"

A great cheer rose from the sailors.

With a grinding of chains, the fleet put anchor in a glistening cove. Co-lumbus and some of his men rowed ashore. Carlos perched proudly on the Ad-miral's shoulder and looked eagerly about.

Columbus had spoken often of the treasures of the East — palaces with roofs of gold, gardens fragrant with rare spices, cloth of jewel-toned silk.

Carlos saw none of these things. He saw only a deserted beach, a lush forest alive with the wild, croaking calls of strange and colorful birds. Columbus stepped onto the beach, knelt down, then planted the green banner of the Expedition.

"This place shall be called San Salvador," boomed the Admiral. "I claim the land in the name of Queen Isabella and King Ferdinand of Spain. Thanks be to God."

A small group of people — unclothed, their skin the color of cinnamon — shyly crept from the forest.

"We come in peace," Columbus assured them, holding up his hand. They did not understand. They began to smile, though, when Columbus gave them gifts of hawks' bells, little red caps, and glass beads. In exchange, the natives gave him spears, cotton thread, and cassava bread made from a plant called the manioc.

Columbus named the people Indians, for he was certain he had reached the Indies. Soon the natives understood that the Spaniards were looking for gold.

The Indians told Columbus they would show him where to find gold. Before he set sail again, a small girl gave the Admiral another gift. It was a strange bird called a parrot.

"A beauty, a treasure!" Columbus declared loudly, and held the parrot aloft for all his men to see. Its rainbow feathers shone like rubies, emeralds, and sapphires.

"He will join us on our search for gold and glory," said the Admiral.

"Gold and glory," croaked the parrot in a voice that rattled like old bones.

Carlos huddled on Columbus's shoulder. He felt very small and plain compared to the bright, raucous parrot.

Paddling a hollowed-out log, the natives led Columbus's ships from island to island. For two months he explored the new lands.

Carlos tasted the water of salt lagoons and heard the hum of jewel-breasted birds no bigger than a man's thumb. Columbus discovered rivers and waterfalls. He met peaceable natives and fierce ones. He saw wonders no Spaniard had ever seen before.

But he found little gold.

On Christmas, in a port the Admiral called La Navidad, the *Santa Maria* ran aground and was wrecked. Columbus made the *Nina* his flagship, for the *Pinta* had sailed elsewhere in search of gold.

"It is time to go back to Spain," the Admiral said one evening. "I must tell Queen Isabella what I have found. We will bring some of the natives and our friend the parrot to show the people of Spain."

"Another bird," growled Don Gato. "Who needs another bird?" Arching his back and bristling his fur, the cat hissed. Carlos clung fearfully to his perch. The parrot screeched loudly. Don Gato slunk under the chart table.

Perhaps, thought Carlos, this new bird is useful after all.

On the voyage back to Spain, the ships had to fight a storm so fierce that Columbus feared they would all drown. Thunder raged and rain lashed the *caravelas*. Waves as high as houses swept the decks. The ships bobbed liked corks in a bucket. Even the seasoned sailors groaned with sickness. Carlos prayed he'd not fall too close to Don Gato.

Columbus sealed a letter in a barrel and set it adrift, so that others would learn of his great discovery if he did not survive the storm.

But he did survive, and all his men with him. The *Nina*, her sails tattered, her hull leaking, reached Spain on March 15, 1493.

"Home!" sang Carlos, flitting high above the crowds gathered at the wharf. "We are home!"

"It's about time," snarled Don Gato. His teeth gleaming, he sprang at Carlos.

Before the cat's claws could sink into Carlos, the parrot swooped down from the ratlines and pecked Don Gato's head. Grateful and relieved, Carlos flew to safety.

"This is not *my* home," said the parrot in his rattly voice. He cocked a bright eye at Don Gato. "I'll be back on this ship soon, cat," he warned.

"Carlos!" the Admiral said. "You must come with me to Barcelona to tell the Queen about our great voyage of discovery."

Carlos did not want to go to Barcelona. He did not want to meet the Queen. He wanted to go home to Gabrielo.

But the Admiral of the Ocean Sea was looking at him with his deep blue eyes and calling to him in his clear, rich voice. Carlos remembered that he belonged to Columbus now. He did not want Columbus to take back the one hundred *maravedis* he had given old Gabrielo.

So Carlos perched on the Admiral's shoulder, the parrot perched on the
other, and they traveled in a grand procession for eight hundred miles.

In Barcelona, Queen Isabella and King Ferdinand received Columbus
with great rejoicing.

"Your Majesties," said Columbus, bowing so low that Carlos and the parrot nearly fell from his shoulders. "I have found the way to the Indies. I have
claimed vast lands in the name of Spain." Tears of joy streamed down the Admiral's face.

The King and Queen bestowed wealth and honors on Columbus. They ex-
claimed over the bewildered natives and the beautiful parrot.

"And this," said Columbus, stroking Carlos's tailfeathers, "is my little mascot. He was the first of us to reach land."

Queen Isabella beamed. "For that, he deserves a fine reward." Carlos puffed out his yellow chest and chirped proudly.

Columbus took Carlos onto his finger. "Our voyage together is over, little friend," he said. "I am glad you came with me, to sing sweetly when the men complained and the weather got rough."

Columbus smiled, a smile as wide as the Ocean Sea. "The Queen's reward will keep your friend Gabrielo comfortable for the rest of his days. He'll never have to mend shoes again."

The Admiral turned his eyes west, into the setting sun. "I must make more voyages, discover more lands, and find more gold for Queen Isabella and King Ferdinand."

"More?" Carlos squeaked in dismay. "More?" For him, one adventure was enough.

"I will take my friend the parrot on the next voyage," Columbus continued. "And you, little Carlos, you must fly away home."

The Admiral held Carlos high in the air and, calling a fond farewell, launched him upward.

Carlos soared to the sky, and his heart soared even higher. "Goodbye," he sang to the Admiral of the Ocean Sea. "Goodbye!"

When he reached Palos and the cobbler's silent shop, Gabrielo was nap-
ping.

Carlos hopped onto Gabrielo's head, then onto his shoulder.

Startled, the old cobbler awoke. "Carlos! I thought I'd never see you
again."

"I'm home," cooed Carlos. "Home."

"Did you find your gold and glory?" the cobbler asked gently. His old eyes spoke a silent message of happiness.

"Gold and glory," Carlos sang. He swooped joyfully around the shop.

A royal messenger brought a chest full of riches. People arrived from far and wide to see the brave little bird who had found gold and glory for Spain.

But Carlos had found much more. He'd sailed west with the wind. He'd seen new lands, new peoples. He'd helped the Admiral of the Ocean Sea open a new world.

But now he was home, and that was the happiest place to be.

Afterword

Columbus's moment of glory didn't last. He made four more voyages to the lands he called the Indies, and didn't realize he'd found a new world until his third voyage. He became Viceroy of the Indies, but he was not as good at governing as he was at discovering. In 1506, at the age of fifty-four, he died in Valladolid, Spain. History has proven him the greatest explorer of them all.

Sources

The author's principle sources for the factual information in this
book are:

Fulson, Robert, translator. *The Log of Christopher Columbus*. Camden, ME: International Marine Publ. Co., 1987.

Granzotto, Gianni. *Christopher Columbus: The Dream and the Obsession*. Garden City, NY: Doubleday, 1985.

Morison, Samuel Eliot. *Admiral Of the Ocean Sea*. Boston: Little, Brown & Co., 1942.